to Sara,

Enjoy the Journey !

Best Wishes
Jeanne Le Seur

Whispers from the Past

Jeanne LeFevre

ISBN 0-7414-2844-X

Published by:

INFINITY
PUBLISHING.COM

1094 New DeHaven Street, Suite 100
West Conshohocken, PA 19428-2713
Info@buybooksontheweb.com
www.buybooksontheweb.com
Toll-free (877) BUY BOOK
Local Phone (610) 941-9999
Fax (610) 941-9959

Printed in the United States of America

Printed on Recycled Paper

Published January 2006

Author's note

May the undying Presence that surrounds this book
follow me through these pages. May the ideas—that
are above, below, and around me—flow through me
and become alive through the written word. I ask that
the possibilities that are only available to those, whose
reach is far beyond their grasp, be given to this writer's
outstretched hands.

Acknowledgments

Every once in a while, life hands us a gift. The following people have been that gift to me, in accomplishing a lifelong dream. With a thankful heart, I dedicate this book:

To my husband, Jeffrey, who graciously allowed me to call his character Andrew. He has been the greatest enthusiast of my book and the most loving husband for thirteen years. I could not have written this book without him. I love you always. Lovingly, to my daughters—Cheryl, Kimberly, and Jill—otherwise known as Emma, Olivia, and Lilly. They have not only been an inspiration to their characters, but also a true inspiration to me all of their lives. I am proud to be their mother. To my mother, Anna, who has always encouraged me to move forward. I love her and thank her for that. To my father, grandparents, Joe, Patsy, and Ed. Their spirits are very much a part of this book. To Jace, my remarkable little Jacob. To Linda, who reminds me of Maggie. To Max, Barney, and Scrappy—my faithful friends, who listened to my ideas late into the night, skipped a few meals, and donated their walking time. To my graphic designer, Mikey Gudikunst, who made my book come alive through his visual expression. To my editor, a special thank-you for teaching me the English language. To my publisher, who ushered my book into print.

To the spirit that lives in all of us.

Table of Contents

PROLOGUE

I am the owner of a small bookstore in a little hamlet in New England. I sell old books, rare books, used books, and I have some copies of books that are no longer in print. I have a passion for books, and although I have never written one, I have read many and have helped young writers publish their manuscripts when major publishing companies rejected them. I tell you, the reader, this because after all the years in this business, I believe I know books and writers quite well, and I could recognize a unique story when I read one. The original text of one such story still sits on an old wooden bookshelf in the back of my store. It fell into my hands quite unexpectedly when a young couple delivered an envelope to me. It was a beautiful fall morning, as I sat at my desk in the back room of my shop. The chimes, fastened to the old wooden door, announced their arrival, and I walked to the front to greet them. They introduced themselves and told me that they had just purchased the old Victorian house that was situated on a little farm just outside of town. They had bought the home at an estate sale and were told that the owner was an unmarried woman, a teacher, who recently died. She requested in her Last Will and Testament that the home be sold and the money distributed to her nieces and nephews.

The couple said that as they were storing some of their belongings, they had discovered a large sealed envelope behind a rebuilt partition in the far corner of the attic. They thought that it was odd to have found it there. They would have returned the packet to the woman's family, but my name and the address of this bookstore were printed on the envelope. For that reason, they believed that the previous owner of the old house wanted me to have it, and so they came here today to deliver it. The couple apologized for being in such a hurry, but they were meeting with a craftsman who would be helping them restore the house, and they were anxious to be on their way. I thanked them, and they left.

As I looked at the envelope, I wondered why I had received it. I was familiar with the location of the estate. Occasionally, I would hear conversation about the beautiful flower and herb gardens surrounding the property, and the elderly woman who lovingly cared for them. Recently, I heard the woman had died, and the news of her death brought to mind my first and only meeting with her. I remember she came into the bookstore one day in search of a volume about raising and caring for herbs. She especially wanted to have the book include Chamomile, Lavender, and Rosemary. I believe her name was Sophia. It was a long time ago, and although the memory of our conversation has dimmed over the years, I can still remember the kind and gentle look in her eyes. Her graying hair, which was braided and pinned into a bun on the back of her head, gave her a very dignified appearance. I recall that she was a small, thin woman, with features that led me to believe that she may have been very beautiful in her younger years. Still confused about the envelope in my hand, I took the packet to the back of the store and sat down at my desk. I broke the seal and removed what I thought to be an old journal. The pages were yellowed and tattered. On the bottom of the last page, the name *Sophia* was written. Bewildered, I stared at the book for a few minutes, and then I was moved to do something I never did before. I closed the store in mid-morning during my usual business hours. Walking to the front of the store, I turned the sign to "closed" and pulled down the door shade. As I walked back to my desk, I stopped and glanced around the store. I had the feeling that I was not alone; yet, for some odd reason, the sensation was not disturbing to me. I settled into my old worn chair and once again, I picked up the journal and started to read….

With book in hand, the hours passed…. With great curiosity, I continued to read it…. With great hesitation, I started to believe it…. then, with a humbling respect for a woman I barely knew, I vowed to publish the following pages in her honor.

Introduction

"The Journal"

My name is Sophia. Twenty years ago, at age fifty-five, I purchased an old Victorian farmhouse located on the outskirts of a small New England town. I bought it at an estate sale that had been advertised on a bulletin board in an antique shop in the little town where I lived. The ad inadvertently fell from the wooden board, as I was speaking with the shopkeeper. She was about to discard it, when, for some reason, the picture of the old house caught my eye, and I asked her if I could look at it. Always wanting to own an old house, I decided to investigate the property. The house was situated on many acres of woodland with a stone barn, a large cornfield, beautiful flower and herb gardens, and a little running stream. A dirt road separated it from the rest of the countryside. The previous owner was an elderly woman who recently died, and her children were not interested in keeping the property. As soon as I saw it, I wanted to buy it, and because the price was right, I soon became the new owner of an old farmhouse.

At first, I thought I bought it because I fell in love with the Victorian architecture as well as the original structures in the house. As time went by and I lived there for a while, I realized that it was much more than that. I loved it because I felt oddly connected to it. I remember, that when I first saw the old home, I had a longing to live there that, strangely, I couldn't explain. It was that same yearning that I soon realized connected me with the untouched oldness that each room held and, surprisingly, the woman who lived there all of her life.

I met this woman through an old trunk I found in the attic. The day I moved in, I had placed some cartons filled with my possessions in front of a worn partition in the far corner of the attic. Because I did not have the time to open the boxes immediately, I simply marked them, "to be open at a later date." One year later, I returned to the task when I was granted a teaching sabbatical. During that time, the weight of the cartons must have taken their toll against the wall; for when I moved the last box to unpack it, the partition collapsed. An old wooden trunk stood behind the crumbled wall. It seemed odd to have found it standing there. I had explored the attic many times and had no recollection of ever seeing it before. It reminded me of a small treasure chest. Made out of wood, it had a slightly domed top with worn leather straps, and although it showed evidence of age, it seemed to display a rather stately pose. I thought, at first, I would continue unpacking my things and explore the trunk later, but for some reason, my attention seemed to be drawn back to the chest. I wondered if it belonged to the previous owner and was accidentally overlooked by her children when they sold the house. Curious about what I would find, I slowly walked toward the trunk until I stood directly in front of it.......

That is when I met this spirit for the first time. As I reached for the trunk, it seemed like unseen hands welcomed me, and a faint whispering voice invited me to open it. Bewildered, I brushed away the dust and cobwebs. Then, with some reluctance and hesitation, I unfastened the old leather straps. Slowly, I raised the lid of the trunk. The contents revealed a musty odor that I soon realized came from many tied bundles of papers and letters as well as pictures, cards, and objects. Looking around the attic, I felt that I was not alone; yet I did not seem afraid of what may be a mysterious caller. As a young girl, my grandmother had always taught me about the spiritual nature of life. I grew up believing that the events in our lives happened for a reason, and many times, it was the peculiar that connected the event to the reason. Unexpectedly finding the trunk, I wondered if it contained a message for me. Many thoughts rushed through my mind. Just like a roulette wheel that spins and slowly stops on a given number for an unknown reason, it seemed like my mind, in similar fashion, was gradually halted on a random thought. In that thought, there was little doubt that this trunk was left here for me to discover, and perhaps the reason was in the timeliness of the discovery. For years, I had made feeble attempts to take some time away from my teaching career, but I always found an excuse not to do so. Then one year after purchasing the old house, I had a change of heart. For some reason, I was ready to take some time to think about my life and the direction I was going. Shortly after that, the teaching sabbatical was granted. Looking back, I believe the timing of the sabbatical and the discovery of the trunk were connected.

My grandmother would tell me that when we are ready to become the student and learn about the things that really matter in life, a teacher would be sent to us to show us the way. Although I embraced her accepted wisdom, I was rather skeptical that it would ever happen to me.

Suddenly, the thought of something unknown directing my path, frightened me. I instinctively stood up and moved away from the trunk. I dismissed the idea of a spirit by blaming it on fatigue or my vivid imagination. The notion to close the trunk and return it to its hiding place made good sense. I was about to do this, when this force, whatever it was, became relentless in capturing my attention to follow it. Was it the spirit of the woman who lived here before? Was she leading me in some direction? I did not know. The only thing I was sure of was the uncertainty of the destination.

It was early December, and the snow lay silently on the slate attic roof. As I stared at the contents of the trunk, I still did not understand why our two paths had crossed. It wasn't until later in my life that I fully realized the secret. On that late fall morning, in the quiet humble spaces of an old attic, a teacher stood before her student, and the lesson to be learned was at hand. I carried the trunk across the attic and placed it on top of an old dusty cedar chest that my aunt had given to me. My first impulse was to empty the trunk and organize

8

the tied bundles, for there seemed to be no logical order to what was inside. As I started to do this, my eyes became fixed on an old photograph of a woman in her later years. She was a stranger to me, only in the respect that I had never met her before, although her eyes held a familiarity that I recognized at once. As I gazed at her picture, then looked down at the trunk, I realized that this treasure was far beyond a world of organization. There was no need for logic. I would walk the path that I felt she had prepared for me, and perhaps, quietly and patiently, she would tell me what she wanted me to hear. In her eyes, I recognized a woman of great strength and inner beauty. In a sense, she was a woman I could only imagine, yet a self that I had searched for through many of my years. I decided I would read the bundle that my hand was led to first, and I would continue in that pattern as I followed her on this passage. In this way, maybe I would understand the reason that we were brought together, and hopefully, the journey would take on a momentum of its own.

BUNDLE ONE

In the beauty of the evening
Comes the memory of the day
In the silence of the nighttime
As we bow our heads and pray
We remember all the footsteps
Of our path along the way
In the beauty of the evening
Comes the memory of the day

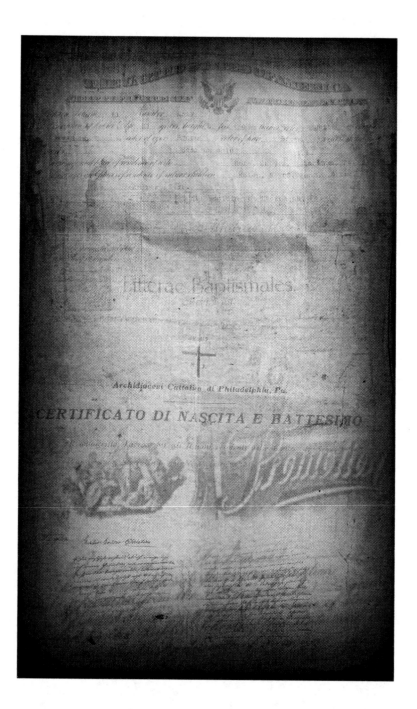

The first bundle was thin, and it sat directly on top of all the others, like it was placed there on purpose. I believe that this spirit wanted to be introduced formally and properly, for the bundles contained legal documents and information. Under her photograph was a yellowed birth certificate. From that, I discovered that her name was Emily. As I stared at the document, I was immediately reminded of the death certificate that her daughters presented at the closing of the estate sale. It showed that she had died at the age of 95. She was an educated woman, for a college diploma from a small woman's college in New England and a graduation hat tassel were folded neatly under her birth certificate. I discovered a marriage certificate with a tiny gold band taped to it. I could only imagine it celebrated a blessed union somewhere in her late twenties. Three birth certificates, that were tied in a thin strand of frayed pink ribbon, announced the arrival of three baby daughters throughout her thirties. Along with the photograph, all these things started to reveal a woman who lived and loved for just a time. These papers that appeared to be frequently stroked by hands and aged by time were separated from the last page in the bundle by what appeared to be two handmade ornaments. Under the ornaments was a poem:

Time Remembered

A new day awakens, the early morn is near
I'll light the stove shortly, for winter is here

The old house is quiet as I creep down the stairs
To my rocker that's placed by the window with care

The land looks so barren when fall comes to a close
With snowflakes falling, as the winter wind blows

Out in the cornfield, a few deer I see
A cardinal and bluebird playing games in a tree

I'll sit here awhile, and celebrate the time
It's the day before Christmas, and I'm age eighty-nine

As I look out the window, I remember the day
When I was much younger, and had children at play

The day used to be busy, preparing the feast
And the children excited, would get under my feet

They were waiting for Santa, and pleaded to see
Inside the big presents, wrapped under the tree

I remember the choosing of each gift that we packed
Each one held a meaning—each one specially wrapped

The children made ornaments…. an angel…. an elf
Once they hung on the tree, now they sit on the shelf

I saw the lit candles, and felt the warmth of the day
I heard all the singing, and saw the games we played

I remember the good times, I also remember the sad
When this season stole away, the very best that I had

He was the love of my life, and God took him away
His hand slipped from mine on a lone winter's day

Oh yes! we had our times, on a day such as this
We decorated the tree, and we hugged and we kissed

Then we waited for family, with gifts and candy galore
We spoiled the grandbabies, who came to our door

The years were all good ones, as I sit and recall
Now his presence is near, I feel his hand on my shawl

As I walk to the living room, he follows after me
And together, once more, we place the star on the tree

"I will always be with you," I heard him gently say
"And especially tomorrow your favorite, Christmas Day"

Then softly I whispered, "I know you are here
To hold me and love me, and partake in our cheer"

For tomorrow, they'll visit, the family we adore
And our home will be filled with Christmas once more.

Emily

A stillness came over me that was only disturbed by an urge to run my hands over the ornaments that were in the trunk. I could barely distinguish what they were, but in my mind's eye, I saw the angel and the elf that she described in the poem. Over the years, she must have saved these treasures and lovingly hung them on the tree each Christmas.

After reading the poem, I felt compelled to trace her steps down the back stairway to the kitchen. Using the poem as my guide, I started down the old wooden attic steps. I had walked up and down them a hundred times since I moved into the house, but this time it was different. This time, I was not alone. In front of me walked a woman in an old woolen housecoat with worn slippers on her feet. Her hair was braided down her back, but loosened from what may have been a restless night of sleep. The house was still quiet and cold when we reached the kitchen. Trying to renew the day, I walked over to the old gray stove that had not been fired for years, since my attempts in the past to light the stove had been unsuccessful. Next to it, sat a bucket filled with coal that I left there for decoration. Carefully, I opened the lid. Then, as if a hand was helping me lift the bucket, I poured the coal into the stove. With a single match, the stove was lit. Then the spirit motioned for me to sit down in the rocker next to the kitchen window. As I looked out, I realized what she saw, as she looked out that same window on a late fall day many years ago. Two winters had gone by, and I wondered why I had never noticed this view before. The snow was falling gently, and the land looked barren. The birds were playing, and a few deer were out in the cornfield, looking for what might be their last good meal for the winter. For some reason, I started to recall my childhood days around Christmas.

It was my favorite day of the year. I remember my mother and my father. I remember the race with my brother and sister on Christmas morning that started in our bedrooms and ended in front of the Christmas tree in our parlor. Later in the day, our family would gather together around the dinner table to enjoy a feast and celebrate the holiday. For the first time, I was seeing it from a mother's eyes. I started to read the poem again, but it seemed like it was being read to me. My mother must have felt the same way as Emily did, and had the same longings after Dad died and we grew up and went our way. She must have missed us so much. It made me realize how insensitive I was at times to my mother's feelings, and I was saddened by the thought. Suddenly, I was distracted by the scent of wax candles. When I turned around to see if any were burning in the house, I saw another spirit slowly approaching.

Like a mother reaching for her child, Emily's hand gently slipped over mine. She seemed to sense the fear that was building up within me, and perhaps she wanted to comfort me. This spirit, who I believed to be her husband, gently put his arm around her shoulder, and together, we walked to the living room. A large pine tree stood in the corner. This year, I had found a perfect Christmas tree in the woods behind the house. I cut it down early, and brought it in the house so I could enjoy the pine scent during December. It was the first time that I had a Christmas tree since I moved into this house, and it looked beautiful in the corner of the living room. Not having the time to decorate it, the tree remained bare. Then the spirits extended their hands toward it, and in an instant, it was covered with small bubbling candle lights and painted Santa ornaments from long ago. In her hand, she held a gold star that she and her husband were about to place on the top of the tree. She drifted from my side to take her husband's hand, and I could hear them gently whispering words of love and longing for each other.

I had remained single during my life, and perhaps so preoccupied with my teaching career, that I never experienced the depth of love that they displayed for each other. In that moment, I felt their pain of separation when he died, her acceptance to remain with their children until God called her home, and her vision of being with him upon her death. I felt certain that they were as one now, and he was holding her and loving her as he did during their lifetime together in this house.

I must have left them in the living room, for I found myself rushing back to the attic, in the hope of learning more about this man that meant so much to Emily.

BUNDLE TWO

When we hold our hands together

We create a symphony

And the music that emerges

Is the song of you and me

We sing it oh! So softly

Yet it echoes in the breeze

When we hold our hands together

We create a symphony

When I untied the white satin ribbon that held this bundle together, it revealed a worn black booklet. A yellowed college diploma, and a picture of a man, known as Andrew, was attached to the document. There was a short newspaper clipping that contained information about him and introduced me to this man. He also graduated from a college in New England. I started to imagine that Emily and Andrew met each other in a little New England town during their college years and fell in love. His course of study and his life's work must have been that of a physician, because the letters MD followed his name. There were other newspaper clippings applauding his work in their community and honoring his accomplishments among his professional colleagues. In the back of the booklet, there was a collection of poems and a few cards that looked like they had been kept for years. There was a picture of a young couple holding hands and smiling at each other. On the bottom of the photograph was written, "Just a man, loving just a woman, for just a time." As I started to read the cards, I discovered a woman that loved her husband, and marked their time through her handmade remembrances to him. I also met a man who intimately and completely loved his wife, his best friend.

Dear Emily,

On Our Anniversary

Some years ago, we married in a small chapel, and it was a time for us to hold dear. We honeymooned in New Hampshire........Remember our time. The nights by the fire and the fine wine we shared.

My love,

Tomorrow is tomorrow, but we have today, and it is a gift to us. Let you and I use this time to live, love, and play. I know, Emily, I have said it again and again, but today, let me tell you once more that you are my dear Wife, my Life, and my best Friend.

Andrew

An old dried red rose lay folded in the letter.

Andrew!

My dear, dear, husband, I love you.

With my hand in your hand

With my heart tucked in yours

Our steps walk together

Our love opens doors.

Emily

I put the letter down, and I started to rummage through the bundle for a wedding picture of this couple. I was anxious to share in the romance, the expression, and the intimacy that this man and woman must have shared on their wedding day.

I was disappointed, for a wedding photograph was not to be found. Instead, I discovered a piece of old lace that I imagined belonged to her wedding dress. I pictured this dress adorning her youthful body during a small and intimate wedding ceremony in the little chapel that he had described in his letter. One dried carnation lay on top of the lace. I guessed that this was the boutonniere he wore on his suit, and his mark of respect to her on their day. A string of stained pearls and a gold watch, that no longer worked, but marked the time of three o'clock in the afternoon, was tightly packed in the pocket of the booklet. Did the watch just stop at three, or did this woman chronicle the time of their wedding ceremony? Were the pearls a wedding gift to her? Was the watch a remembrance for him? Again, I desperately wanted to find a wedding picture. I even thought about calling the family and asking if there was one available for me to see. Her daughter had given me her phone number at the sale of the house, and I remember putting it away in case I would need it at a later date. Eagerly, I ran to the attic steps and began to hurry down to my room to look for my phone book......

Perhaps she really did stand in front of me, or maybe I just imagined it, because, suddenly, I stopped. I looked down at the contents of this black booklet, and I knew that everything I needed for this journey with her was already in front of me. As it sometimes happens, one loses sight of the quiet message of the spirit when the mind insists on working alone and occupying itself with the unimportant. I realized that what I was searching for could not be found in a photograph. There was something with deeper meaning before me, and I needed to be patient in order to find it. A gift was waiting for me at the end of the journey, but my heart had to be prepared to receive it. I felt that the spirit of this woman was chosen to lead me in a direction that I avoided most of my life. Perhaps the contents of the trunk would help me reach that destination.

In that moment, I believed that she was destined to be my teacher long before she died, and I believed that we sought each other, long before we met. I sometimes wonder if the spirit just waited for the right time to embrace me—for the timing was perfect. Like the unraveling of a blossom that, under the Divine Law of the universe, does not open one moment sooner then it is called to do so. This was my journey with her, and I welcomed it. I wanted to know more about her and this man she loved. I had an idea I was about to find out.

To My Husband on Valentine's Day

It's Valentine's Day—that Day of the year
When two hearts together can eagerly peer
Into the future—Where will love go?
Take hold of my hand, and soon we will know

Starting our life, we were young, we were gay
We smiled and laughed and loved as we may
"Let's take our ideas, and move them along
We have happiness and health and even a song"

But move as it may, life will pass ever so fast
And later we'll sit and smile at the past
We will rock in our chairs, where once we would glide
As you draw up your rocker and sit by my side

For although age has made us unsteady and weak
We still reach for each other, each other we seek
You pull at my hand, mine leans to yours too
Forever remembering all that we do

As the breeze sways the rockers, we laugh as we think
Of sunsets and moonlights, winters and springs
They sure brought the good times, for me and for you
When the family all gathered, and the dog loved it too

And no matter how busy we somehow would get
We always touched lovingly, when our eyes met
It's late and you'll tell me, good night, we must go
But oh, my good husband, I want you to know

Before we will sleep, I must tell you this
Please hear me, my love, so it won't go amiss
For when you and I are summoned to rest
By that "Great Old Someone" who says, He knows best
I want you to know that my dream has come true
For during my life, I have been loved by you

Emily

The poem that I held in my hand was beautiful. I closed my eyes and started to think about Emily and Andrew sitting in their rockers on the porch and holding hands.....Then suddenly, it occurred to me; My God, I still have those old rockers. I remember painting them green when I found them in the old summer kitchen last year. They were broken in places, and I had them repaired. Then I put them on the front porch.

Running down the steps into the kitchen, I flung open the front door that led to the porch. Suddenly, I stopped. The green rockers were sitting there side by side, but this time they were not empty. Two middle-aged people were sitting in them on what seemed to be a summer's evening. They were holding each other's hand. They were laughing and talking at the day's end. They were holding teacups and enjoying the evening. My first impulse was to join them, but I was afraid that they would disappear if I moved closer. Was it the vision that brought about the feeling, or the feeling that triggered the vision? I'm just not sure. I only knew, at that moment, I was filled with an awareness from somewhere that the greatest gift one might possess is to give love and receive love back. Throughout my life, I believed that love came easy, and when things got difficult, one simply stopped trying and turned away.

On this summer's evening, as I watched these two people give their time and love freely to one another, I started to see it all differently.

Happy Birthday, Andrew

As you turn 45, on your birthday today
My words turn to wishes in many, many ways

I wish you long life and a long healthful tide
With all that you need, and me at your side

I wish for you strength—inside and out
And belief in yourself, without ever a doubt

I wish for you wealth, that you hold in your hand
No more or no less, but enough to withstand

I wish for you laughter, heartfelt and swift
And to give it to others, as a child-like gift

I wish for you quiet, immaculate times
With book, soup, and ladle, and candles of pine

I wish you the wisdom of a strong, creative mind
To succeed in your work, to be one of a kind

But I wish for you also, the wisdom of age
For that in the end, will complete the final page

And although it sounds strange, I wish you old age
With our family together at the sad final stage

I wish you a peace that penetrates the whole
And uplifts your heart, and unleashes your soul

So as you collect this Wishes Bouquet
Gather also my love on your Special Day.

Emily

Dearest Emily,

I will love you always. You have been my inspiration. I have shared so much of myself with you, and you have helped me walk in places where I have been unsure. I have risen to more challenges than I ever thought I could. You have changed my life. You are my life. I love you deeply and forever.

Andrew

Each card that she sent to him was handmade and had some type of cross-stitch or embroidery on it. Most of the time, the script in her correspondence was done in calligraphy. It almost looked like she selected memories by choosing letters and cards that she wanted to keep. I suppose by keeping too many, it interrupted the intimacy, and by keeping too few, the complete story of two people in love could not have been told. The remembrances were not special life markers like a fiftieth birthday or a twenty-fifth wedding anniversary; rather, she chose ordinary moments that had extraordinary meaning for her and Andrew—the quiet subdued evening of their wedding anniversary, or the Valentine's day celebration on the front porch rocking chairs while enjoying a peaceful sunset. These were their distinctive tributes to each other. I think that she wanted to leave the memory of a marriage that was a blend of separate strength and connected love. I think that she wanted to show that this kind of love could be celebrated on any day of their lives, in the simplest fashion. They didn't mark a day; rather, they marked a marriage. They truly needed each other. I feel that sometimes she led and he followed, then sometimes he took the lead, and she followed. There must have been times when she gave him wings to fly higher than he believed he could, or times when he let her stand on his shoulders, so she could see beyond her stature and myopic vision. It was my perception that they encouraged each other in their dreams and hopes and sustained each other in their difficult times. Although some dreams may have faded, I sensed that they were always replaced with new ones, and that their day-to-day living and loving transformed a relationship into a lifelong commitment.

It all felt so real. Back in the attic, I placed the black book and cards in the trunk, and once again, her presence was near.

As I reached for the third bundle, her hand descended over mine, and strangely, the emotion ebbed from contentment into sadness.

BUNDLE THREE

In the living of our life
The joys and sorrows that we know
In the dying of the body
Comes the unveiling of the soul
As we lay our heads so softly
In the Arms that won't let go
In the dying of the body
Comes the unveiling of the soul

You will feel His peace and comfort
On a night you search for rest
You will feel His loving Presence
On a day you call your best
From the infant in the cradle
To the elder on death's bed
You will feel His peace and comfort
On a night you search for rest

As I untied the worn silk ribbon, my hand rested on an envelope. "Found in the jacket pocket of his favorite suit" was written with a pencil on the outside of the envelope. Except for the black ribbon, I had no idea why I was filled with grief, until I opened the envelope and started to read the letter.

My Dearest Emily,

I want you to know that you are, and always have been, the most important person and influence in my life. You were always on my mind, and on my mind in all ways. Life does not hold much promise for us, Emily, if we cannot dream, and so, I had my dream. The essence of that dream was you; therefore, it means so much to me, at this time, that you embrace what I am about to say.

I'm sorry that you did not receive this letter from me sooner. Please forgive me, but I could not find a good way to say good-bye. The day I started this letter was the day you brought me home from the hospital, and I could no longer get out of bed. I knew my remaining time with you was brief. That night, I prayed that God would give me one more day to live, and be in command of my senses, so I could write this letter to you. I then had it placed where I knew you would find it upon my death, since we agreed that I would be buried in my favorite suit. Remember the one you bought for me as a gift a few years ago when I wanted the fishing rod and you felt I needed a suit more? I am thankful for that suit now, for it provided a place to deliver this letter to you, and it is a part of you that I will take with me. Emily, if you are reading this letter, I know you are crying. I felt it too. I thought the pain of my illness was unbearable, but I realized that it was nothing compared to the agony I suffered when I knew death was about to separate us. As time goes by, perhaps you can replace the tears with some smiles when you think about the wonderful memories of you and me. My sweetheart, the dance was perfect. If I had to write a life script for myself, I could not have written a better one. I could not imagine what my life would have been like without you. How quickly it all went by. One day, we were saying hello at the college library, and the next day, we are saying good-bye at the bedside that we shared for forty years. Thank you for all the days in between. The simplicity of our life together was beautiful. I love you deeply and completely.

Do not ever be afraid, for I will love you and watch over you from where I am going. I will make the journey first. That is the way it should be, my love, so that when God calls you, simply hold out your hand, and you will feel mine taking hold of yours. I will be waiting for you.

Emily, I want you to know that you will be my last conscious thought..........

Andrew

I don't know how long I sat there with the letter on my lap, but the light was fading from the attic window as I folded the letter and placed it back in the envelope. I imagined she cried as she read it many times, because the letter was worn thin and the ink was stained. According to the attached death certificate, Andrew was sixty-eight when he died. The cause of his death was listed as cancer and dated 10 January at 1:05 a.m. The year was blurred. Under the letter from Andrew, there were a few other letters and three pages that looked like they were torn out of a personal diary. Since the light was dimming in the attic, I placed Andrew's letter lovingly back into the trunk and closed the cover. I tucked the unread ones in my pocket and headed down the stairs to my bedroom.

The divan looked comforting, and although an electric light was accessible, I decided to ignite the kerosene lamp instead. As I glanced across the room, my old iron bed appeared to be the only object in view. I started to feel like a visitor in another's home. This room could have been their bedroom. Was it here that they celebrated their love and shared many intimate moments? Is this where she cared for him through his illness? It could have been in this room where they held on to each other and said their last good-bye. I remained motionless. Why did I not sense her presence? Perhaps, the last memory in this room was too tragic for the spirit to revisit. Maybe Emily and Andrew were now together and entwined in each other arms, as Andrew had promised. With some uncertainty, I took the papers out of my pocket.

The first one was written to Andrew from Emily. I was saddened when I thought that Emily was no longer with me, until I started to read aloud the letter dated one year after his death. The words were coming from my mouth, but the voice I heard was hers.

Andrew,

Sometimes thoughts of you seem so real, I almost forget you are not here. Many nights, I sit here and think about you. I miss you terribly. I am writing this letter because it helps put into words what I am going through, and although I cannot hand this letter to you, somehow I know you are reading it. It is beyond my understanding why God chose to take you from me, even though I know that His design is always for our highest good. The days are long, but the nights are eternal, and with each passing year, I move steadily closer to making my way back to you. I yearn for you and desire your kiss and touch. I try to do my best without you every day, but sometimes, living gets so painful that I can only go moment by moment.

I have not changed much in our home since you were taken from me. I need to see the reminders of you constantly, for it is the only way that makes living here without you bearable. I visit those lovely memories often, and in the quiet of the night, you will even find me smiling, as I relive our time together. The music box you gave to me sits on the table next to my chair in the parlor. As I am writing to you, Andrew, I raise the silver cover, twist the turn key, and it is now playing our favorite love song. Do you recall when we danced to that song right here in our parlor? That was a memorable night. As memorable as our vacations at the seashore were after the children moved away. They were romantic times for us, and I only wish we could have shared them longer. The children miss you too, Andrew. They love you and know that you gave them the best you had to give. I know you watch over them and their families. They come to see me often, and the grandbabies always hear stories about you. Jacob reminds me most of you. He has your mind, your eyes, and your smile. Perhaps, someday, he will follow in your footsteps. I'm longing for you today. Your illness and death came suddenly to us. It was truly an unpredictable moment in our lives, and although I do not question it, I still find it hard to accept. We always believed that God plans for us, and whether we understand it or not, His plan unfolds as it should. To think otherwise, Andrew, I would be planting the seeds of my own madness.

It is now nighttime, and I am getting tired. I must go to sleep. Every night I thank God that you are finally free from the dreadful pain of your illness, and that you are at peace. Someday, we will be at peace together. Good night, Andrew….

Emily

I put the first letter down, and started to read the next. From what I could tell, she had written this one five years after his death.

Dearest Andrew,

I'm sitting on our bench in the herb garden on this beautiful summer's evening, and my thoughts turn to you. I am trying to recreate the feeling when we sat here together after a long day and sipped some fresh herb tea. Your favorite was chamomile, and this year has been perfect weather for the herb to thrive. The small white and yellow flower has just started to bloom, and it is everywhere in the garden. The fragrance is strong. This must be in your honor.

I gaze at the big old tree that hangs over the old stone wall. Do you remember how we use to mark the seasons by the branches of the tree? My favorite was the winter, at dusk, when it held its bare branches high against the darkening sky. Your favorite was spring, when the swollen green buds could be seen in the morning sunlight. The bluebird house is in disrepair, but it still rests on the old tree. It doesn't seem like the birds occupy it anymore. Perhaps they are waiting for the kind hands of the owner that built it to mend it where it is worn.

In the silence of this lovely evening, I am aware of your loving and pervading presence. I turn, expecting to see you, but an empty feeling is all that I am left with. I embrace it because it is an overwhelming sentiment of love that I experience, and that I know. For the time being, this is the best we can do.

Andrew, do you smell the fragrance of the red roses from the rosebushes you planted when we started our life together here? They are on the far end of the herb garden, but tonight a strong scent drifts toward me. You were always so proud of those roses and would choose the prettiest one to present to me each year. Soon, I will go over and choose my rose just like you used to do. Tonight, I will place it on the dresser next to your picture. Tonight, it will be my tribute to you. I love you, forever.

Emily

My eyes were filled with tears. The only comfort I felt, after reading the letters, was to believe that talking to Andrew momentarily relieved Emily's pain and longing for Andrew. His death was untimely. I thought of the rose that she placed near Andrew's picture on that night long ago. Somehow, I wished she would have dried it and placed it with this letter, but there was no sign of it between the pages. I sat on the divan, and thoughts of Emily and Andrew filled my mind. I glanced across the room, where I imagined her dresser once stood, and where his picture may have rested.

Suddenly, a delicate scent of roses filled the air. Uncertain of where it was coming from, I moved in the direction of my dresser, but there was no fresh rose in sight. Instead, a vase of dried red roses, which I purchased at the little antique shop the day after I bought the house, stared at me from the far corner of the dresser. Tentatively, I leaned over the vase. The scent grew stronger. In disbelief, I stepped back as I realized the ghostly aroma of fresh roses was coming from the dried bouquet.........

Filled with emotion, I reached into my pocket in search of the other pages. I needed to know more about Andrew's illness and death, for I now had a strong feeling that their last good-bye may have been said in this very room. My notion was correct. As I unfolded the papers, I was staring at three pages from Andrew's journal. One dated around the time that he died.

Mysteriously, as I started to read the words, the scent of roses began to slowly disappear from the room.

04 September

Today, I sit in my friend's office. He is a physician and an old classmate of mine from medical college. I had gone to see him a week ago because of the relentless pain I was having in my stomach. He was thorough with his examination. Today, Emily and I returned to hear the results of the tests. The diagnosis was certain. He had found an advanced cancer in my stomach for which there was no treatment available for him to offer me. I sat there and stared at Emily. I didn't want to believe what I was hearing. His words burned in my head, like a branding iron held against the hide of a helpless steer. Then the words became too painful. The clear voices turned into muffled sounds. I don't know if I just stopped listening, or my brain just stopped accepting what my doctor, my friend, was saying. My thoughts turned to Emily. I hoped she was all right. I prayed for God to be with us.

When we got home, I started to deny it. I thought surely my friend would soon call to tell me that he made a mistake with his diagnosis. Then we could go on with our lives. As the hours passed, my optimism turned to hopelessness, and then to helplessness. My fear was real. My life would never be the same. Where will I find the courage to endure this illness? My eyes turned to Emily. My thoughts turned toward God.

10 October

It is a beautiful Autumn Day. The leaves are at their peak colors, and the children are here to join us for our evening meal. We invited them here tonight to finally tell them about my illness. We tried to wait as long as possible in order to spare them the pain, but the disease is starting to show its outward signs, and our family is asking me how I am feeling a little more than they usually do.

I could feel the silence in the room when I finished speaking. "There is always hope," I said, "but there is no cure for my illness, and that is a reality that we all must accept." They asked no questions tonight, and I am grateful for that. They are crying. I'm sure once they realize what I have said, questions will arise. I gaze at the grief seen on my children's faces. This momentarily suspends the cancerous pain that constantly lives in my abdomen. Tonight, the pain is in my heart. Their faces become silent images in the twilight of the evening, and an agony, that I never thought was possible, fills my soul. Later that evening, after taking my pain medicine, I started to drift off to sleep on my chair in the study. I could hear muffled voices in the next room asking questions to Emily and among themselves. Questions that their minds struggle to answer. Questions that already have answers, but they are unwilling, and unready, to hear.

Oh Emily! You are so strong. Thank you. Thank you.

My children, please hear me.

Dear Children,

I know that you will read this when I am no longer here. My choice was not to leave you, but you must believe that there is a reason that I am being called to God. I love you all as much as I loved life itself. You have brought me so much happiness, and I am proud to be called your father. You are all strong and beautiful women. Your husbands are good men, and our grandbabies are remarkable. They are too young to remember all this, but I know they will know of me from you. I want you to know, I have always tried to do my best for you throughout the years. Those years have passed so quickly. I remember tucking a favorite baby doll into little hands as you fell asleep, and before I knew it, I was placing those beautiful grown hands into your husbands' on your wedding days. I am grateful to have lived as long as I have. I will be with God, and I will watch you from there. Someday, we will all be together again. Do not cry for me. I am with you always. Look for me in the faded shadows......

I love you all and forever.

Father

08 January

Today, I wait for Emily to come and take me home from the hospital. The doctors and nurses can do no more for me, and I thank God my loving family will care for me. It is time for me to go home and prepare for my journey back to God. As a physician, I always tried to heal the human body, although I have always believed that the human body is just a temporary dwelling for the spirit to grow and learn. My purpose and work on earth are finished, and it is time to give up this worn-out body. Cancer has been the vehicle chosen to deliver my spirit Home, and I know that the time is getting closer because the disease is slowly changing my life from the way I once knew it. I made the decision to die as naturally as I was born. I do not want a treatment that will prolong the ending of my life and keep me a prisoner in this cold and informal hospital room. I want to be with my wife and my family, and I am grateful that I can go home and start my final journey from there. I have agreed only to take my pain medicine with me. This elixir is God-sent. It relieves the physical pain, although it only brings a temporary easing of the mental pain that will be part of me until the day I die.

I can hear Emily slowly approaching my door and discussing my illness with the doctor. She is crying. To hear her weep is unbearable. I know that God will give her what she needs to endure this; yet, I search my mind for ways to comfort her when I am no longer by her side. Soon, the nurses will prepare me to go with her. It seems ironic that I have always helped other people, and now I need someone to dress me, help me into a wheelchair, and take me home.

Dear God, be here with me because I cannot do this alone, and be with all who surround me with their love today.

Exhausted and full of grief, I placed the letters aside of me on the divan. My eyes were closed; yet, I have no recollection of sleep. I started to see two images and the vague outline of an iron bed.

He was lying in bed with his hand in hers. I could feel their spirits finding strength in coming together as one and praying to a Higher Being…. a God that would give them the strength they needed when the time came to leave each other… an Eternal spirit that would gently take hold of his hand as it slipped from hers.

She raised her head that was resting on their folded hands. He was lying there, motionless; she was sitting next to him, still cradling his hand. She placed her head next to his cheek and kissed him gently. I could see the tears running down her face on to his. His end was here.

I was crying. I had watched Andrew and Emily share their last human touch. Then, for some reason, my eyes fell on an old clock that rested on a table beside the bed. It announced the same time that was written on Andrew's death certificate....1:05 a.m.

The next morning, the early chirping of birds awakened me. I must have fallen asleep on the divan, for I found myself still lying there. The letters were by my side. I went to the kitchen and prepared some tea. Taking my cup of tea with me, I returned to the attic and Emily's treasure. I retied the letters in the black ribbon, placed them back in the trunk, and reached for the next bundle.

BUNDLE FOUR

I know you are my brother
For I've helped you once before
I carried you to shelter
And laid my back against the door
For when the storm was over
I walked with you once more
I know you are my brother
For I've helped you once before

You reached your hand out to me
When the world went away
I needed arms to comfort
And I needed hands to pray
For there you stayed right with me
'Til I saw the light of day
You reached your hand out to me
When the world went away

Two pictures were the first things I saw when I untied the gold ribbon that secured the fourth bundle. The first picture was that of a woman with the words "Love Maggie" written on the lower right corner. The other picture was of two smiling, young women, with their arms around each other. They were dressed in graduation gowns. The one woman resembled the picture I found of Emily, only younger. The other woman, I think, was Maggie because she looked a lot like the signed photograph. Who was Maggie? I thought.

On the back of the graduation picture, I found the answer to my question. Emily and Maggie were best friends.

Dear Emily,

Graduation Day. We finally did it.

Best Friends Forever,

Maggie

The rest of the bundle contained some letters and cards. A newspaper article and a poem were attached by a tarnished safety pin to a piece of yellowed, waxed paper that enclosed a dried purple flower.

Dear Emily,

There is a sadness about me today because we will be saying good-bye. Our graduation, the professors tell us, is a beginning, and in a way, it is. I am anxious to begin our teaching positions and put into practice what we have learned. It is a beginning, in that we will follow a dream that we were only able to talk about during our years of study. Remember when we first met in the dormitory? Remember how we looked at each other when they told us that we would house together? Timidly, we unpacked our belongings and said little to each other. You were Emily, and I was

Maggie. We wore white blouses and long cotton skirts, and our hair was braided in buns on the top of our heads. Beyond that, we did not know much more about each other. Our friendship grew slowly, but with each step, it led us to a lasting bond that only good friends realize. It was the subtle moments I remember, which brought our lives closer together. Our walks in the deep New England snows when we talked about our dreams, and how we would hope to marry and have children some day. Our chats that lasted into the night, our excitement after the college get-togethers, and all those handsome men we met. The last-minute assignments, the late-night study groups, and all the tests we thought we did not pass were only balanced by the unexpected suitors, the late-night dormitory fun with our friends, and the tests we did pass. Through those years, we took our turn being smart women, scared women, stylish, and clever.

Yes, they are right—we are at a beginning, but we are also at a crossroads. You will be staying here in New England, and I will be moving to the Midwest. Life as we have known it will be changing. Our daily face-to-face conversations will turn into correspondence through the mail, and our time together will have to wait for the next visit. I thank God our paths have crossed.

So today, Emily, I'm trying to say good-bye to you. I have saved a few small remembrances from our college days, and I placed them in a red velvet box in your valise. When you open this letter, after you arrive home, you will find the box. I placed it under the white blouse that I borrowed from you last year for that special date with the man that will soon be my husband. Write to me soon. I hope to see you at our wedding ceremony…. Love, Maggie.

The red velvet was worn and frayed, and the torn cover slipped off the box as soon as I picked it up. Inside, there was a small picture of two little girls walking hand in hand down a flowered path with an inscription at the bottom, "good friends never let go." A tarnished, gold-colored bracelet with tiny rhinestones, one missing, lay curled up at one end of the box. A red and gold hair clip, a lucky quarter, a trolley car token, two tickets from the World's Fair, and a little metal plate that said, "Emily-Maggie-Room 107," finished the tokens of affection. As I held each remembrance in my hand, I felt nostalgia for a past that was not mine. Whether Emily was remembering through me, or the spirit of Maggie was present for a brief moment, I was assured of a strong friendship that started at the beginning of their college years and held the promise of a lifetime. I could only imagine that these women went on to get married, have families and pursue their teaching careers, either formally or informally, whenever they had the opportunity. I was left with the impression that they stayed in touch with each other throughout their entire lives.

I folded the letter and placed it on my lap. With anticipation, I removed the next letter from the envelope. The word *divorce* caught my attention. I stared at the page, not knowing what I was about to read. It was a letter from Maggie to Emily and dated about thirteen years after the graduation message.

Dear Emily,

I know this letter will not come as a shock to you, since we talked about my troubled marriage when we visited each other six months ago. Things between Jonathan and I have only gotten worse. I think that many marriages have their problems, and I also believe that many of those problems have their resolutions. Unfortunately, when they have no resolve, one starts to think about separation and divorce. The last few years for us have not been easy. Love was losing its ground quickly, and we sadly knew that life would be genuinely better for us without each other. Two weeks ago, Jonathan packed his belongings, kissed me good-bye, and left.

The next morning, I awoke alone with this nagging pain in my stomach, and all I could think of was, "What will I do?" I was scared and alone. I wanted to write to you, Emily, because we are always there for each other, but I couldn't even put a pen to paper. Unless you have gone through it, Emily, you cannot understand the isolation and loneliness I was feeling. The only way I could describe it is like standing alone in a glass box, in the middle of a busy city sidewalk, and screaming for help. It feels like everyone passes by, but no one stops. The next day, I visited my doctor, and he said that I was suffering from depression. He called it some sort of depersonalization. I simply call it a cancer in my heart.

The five years spent with Jonathan have left their permanent effects of good and bad. He is a good man, in many ways, but I think we grew apart from each other, and our lives moved in different directions. My strong feelings of insecurity and loss led me to the solitude of my bedroom one night. I was unable to think, to stand, to talk. With a helpless third eye, I watched myself regress. In that room, I cried hysterically and talked to myself until five in the morning. So many thoughts ran through my head. Why did I allow my marriage to get into this situation? Was it me? Was it him? No one was to blame, but it was all so confusing. I always felt that I was a woman of some style, but pitifully crying now, I knew my being knew nothing of style. I thought I was in love when I got married, but today, I feel like I do not even know what the word means.

Every day, I found myself hurting more. I heard it said that when you hurt enough, and you finally get tired of hurting, you change. It's true, Emily. After six months of separation, I hit rock-bottom, then I finally started looking upward. A few days later, I got off my knees and at least tried to stand.

Self-pity is a malignant disease, Emily, and I realize now that the only cure is strong doses of reality. He was gone, and I was alone. The happy ending I was looking for was only to be found in theater and novels, and not in real life. Perhaps, in years to come, it will be easier for me to understand, but for now, I know that I need to start on some sort of convalescence to become whole again. I need to continue on, after this ending.

Thank God there are no children. Perhaps my inability to bear them was an unseen gift from God. Remember, Emily, we always said that He knows what we need before we do. I am sure His plan is unfolding, as it should; therefore, He will give Jonathan and me what we need to endure this hardship.

Today, I know I will survive. A few months ago, I was not sure. Our divorce will be difficult for my family to accept. They always taught me that marriage was forever, and no matter how unhappy one becomes, one stays safely tucked within its discontent. The road ahead will not be easy, but at least I will try to take more time to be open with my thoughts and less disciplined with myself. In my mind, I have taken the sounds of chaos and replaced them with the slow steady ticking sound of an old clock, for I truly believe that only time will heal these open wounds.

I am starting a new teaching position at a women's school near my home. I will visit with you, Andrew, and the children the first chance I get. I hope to see you soon.

Thank you, my dearest friend, for being there for me.

God bless you for all that you are, and all that you do.

With a quiet resignation, I end my letter.

Love, Maggie

For an instant, I could only imagine the feeling that enveloped Emily when she read this letter, and the compassionate words that filled the pages of the return letter to Maggie. I pictured them crying and comforting each other when Maggie came to visit. I felt that they strengthened each other, and continued to love and support each other throughout their lives.

My mind drifted to my own life, and sadness came over me. I realized that I never took the time to have a friendship like that with another human being. I never quite gained the compassion and selflessness that it took to nurture a friendship's lifelong bond. Emily was teaching me. The letters from Maggie to Emily were her guide. She allowed me to be acquainted with two strong women, and in knowing them, learn a gentle lesson—how to love yourself and each other.

The Christmas card was simply beautiful. It was from Maggie to Emily and dated five years after Maggie's divorce. It was hand painted with a gold bond around the edges. A male and female cardinal were nestled in snow-covered Christmas greens that decorated a cozy old front porch. The intensive red color of the male cardinal matched the red bows around the white posts. As one looked into the distance, a picket fence and an old barn surrounded by snow-covered pines could be seen. The sky in the background silently conveyed the stillness of a December morning, just before dawn, when the sky is barely brightening, and life is starting to stir. Inside the card was a lovely Christmas wish for Emily and the family. On the opposite page, there was a short note.

Dear Emily,

Thank you for the warm hospitality when I visited at Thanksgiving. It was wonderful to see everyone, and for us, it was just like old times to be together. Your hug never loses its meaning. It felt the same way it did when we were in school so long ago. I pray our last hug will feel the exact same way. Our friendship extends far beyond appearances. It has a healing power all of its own. Once again, I thank God our paths have crossed.

Andrew is so gracious and loving, and Emma, Olivia and Lilly are growing so beautiful. I enjoyed being with you for that week. I'm sorry I cannot accept your invitation for Christmas, but I have decided to visit with my family and to try to heal some of the old wounds.

I will be fine. I have found a way to give back for the many blessings that have come to me in place of unrealized dreams.

I hope to see you in the spring. I wish you a Merry Christmas and a peaceful and loving New Year.

Love, Maggie

The newspaper article fell when I opened the safety pin. Appearing on my lap was an obituary announcing the death of Maggie. At the top of the page, a picture appeared, and the heading read: *Maggie Hunter, beloved teacher, dies at age 84.* Although the face showed the inevitable signs of age, the smile and the eyes held the firm resemblance of a younger Maggie. The article stated that she was born and raised in the Midwest and went to college in New England where she received a Bachelor of Arts degree, majoring in Education. Her professional teaching career started at a women's college near her home in the Midwest, and there she earned a master's degree and prestigious honors for excellence in her profession. Miss Hunter taught thirty years at the college and was Dean of Education for another ten years, before retiring from her post. She held a strong belief in education for women. She continued to play an active role in maintaining the highest level of academics at the college, after her formal career as an educator ended. She was the author of many published articles and books. All who knew her will remember her wonderful smile and relaxed charm. She succumbed to disease after suffering a heart attack, one week ago. Family and friends were present at her bedside when she passed on.

Attached to the newspaper article was a note that looked like it was torn from a larger journal. It was dated the sixth of May, and Emily's script followed.

Today, my dearest friend died. My friend, Maggie, died today. I don't have words to describe my loss. It is a feeling so heart wrenching that it can no longer be called sadness. It is beyond that. She was someone that was most dear to me, and throughout my life, more than me. We were extensions of each other. We fit together like pieces of a jigsaw puzzle. My children were her children, for she was there through every part of their lives. Her career was my career. She would say I was her other mind that she turned to for advice, encouragement, and support. She smiled with me when my daughters wed, and she cried with me when my husband died. We aged together, but never talked about growing old. We were always those bright young girls that met in college, and we never let that light dim. We possessed thousands of memories. I celebrate her today. I celebrate those memories.

Through this grieving, I find peace because I know she is at peace. Her last week on this earth was spent in a hospital bed, trying to survive the devastation that a heart attack inflicts on a human body. She was ill, but she was never scared. She carried a spiritual beauty about her, and she believed that God would give her the strength she needed either to get well or to start the journey Home to Him. He chose to take her.

I was grateful that I was able to be with her during her last moments and hold on to her hand, until it was tucked tightly in His. We knew when to let go.

I will miss her because I simply love her. I didn't love her because it was right. I just loved her. That is the best of it.

Oh, Maggie, you were right—the last hug was just as good as the first.

A small dried Columbine was nestled inside of the wax paper. I gently held the delicate flower and started to read the poem...An anonymous quotation written out by Elizabeth Lucas.

Do not stand at my grave and weep,

I am not there. I do not sleep.

I am a thousands winds that blow.

I am the diamond glints on snow.

I am the sunlight on ripened grain.

I am the gentle autumn rain.

When you awaken in the morning's hush,

I am the swift uplifting rush of quiet birds in circling flight.

I am the soft star that shines at night.

Do not stand at my grave and cry,

I am not there. I did not die.

I must have fallen asleep; because when I awoke, I was lying on the attic floor. The first signs of early morning were peeping through the small windows, and I could hear the distant sound of a rooster crowing. I remember reading Emily's journal page and holding the newspaper clipping of Maggie's death. The dried Columbine was still in my hand.

I'm not sure how it happened or if it even happened at all. It was like I was waking from a dream—a dream I didn't understand, yet somehow remembered. I relived times in the lives of Emily and Maggie. Somewhere between sleep and wake, I became the spectator of a slide show narrated by these two women, or the spirits of these two women. With them, I walked through the scenes from their lighthearted college days. We were in the college dormitory. The books were piled high on the desk, and the ice skates lay on the closet floor. I walked through the crucial years of their adulthood. I held the crying baby girls with Emily, and stood at the podium of a classroom full of young, enthusiastic students with Maggie. I shared their emotional openness, as they experienced their losses, and celebrated their successes. As they grew older, I sat with them on the front porch rockers when they would visit each other, and I listened to them reminisce—Maggie's visit to England, and Emily's experiences with her grandchildren. I walked with them as they clung to each other at Andrew's funeral, and I stood in the hospital room and watched them cling to each other, as they said their last good-byes before Maggie's passing.

An odd feeling came over me. Was there a reason this was happening to me? Were the spirits of Emily and Maggie just playing? Were they remembering through me, or did they want me to experience the beauty of a strong friendship that lasts until death, and perhaps beyond?

Or was it more than that?

My grandmother always taught me that our spirit chooses to be born into a human form in order to complete the lessons they were given to work on while on earth. Until now, I never gave much thought to this belief. I was fifty-six, and I rarely thought about the reason for my presence on this earth. Now, looking at Emily and Maggie's life together, and then looking at my own life, I felt empty and alone........

Suddenly, I was being given a new way to measure life, and I began to think about my past.

I was a professor in a Massachusetts women's college for twenty-five years, but today, I felt no sense of accomplishment. I taught a class every day. I transferred knowledge, but I never gave anymore than that. I seldom moved beyond the classroom to the human being, to create opportunities for my students to grow personally and to be challenged academically. I neglected my real work and my real purpose. I forgot about giving because I was too preoccupied with getting. I realized I never had a lasting relationship with a man, or a meaningful friendship with a woman. I forgot about loving. I became rooted in the world of unconsciousness and failed to remember my reason for being. Suddenly, I was no longer remarkable in my own eyes. My reflection was insignificant when held up to the contributions and investments that Maggie and Emily made in teaching as well as in life. An awareness so profound was standing in front of me and staring into my soul. The spirit was enveloping me, and I was starting to understand that these happenings were not a coincidence. The visit to the antique shop, finding the house ad, the timing of the sabbatical, the discovery of the trunk, and the appearance of the spirit were astonishing and overwhelming. I was sure that these were not ordinary events, rather a course of undertakings that were prearranged to change the course of my life—to show me how to live each moment to the fullest, with a love and a kindness that asks for nothing in return. To embrace life for others and myself. I was being given a gift so precious and extraordinary. A gift that few are chosen to recognize when the bearer of the offering visits.......

I rose to my feet, and with delight, I held my arms out, like I was hugging the empty space in front of me. To my surprise, the space was not empty at all. Rather a warm loving embrace, by arms I could not see, tenderly encircled me.

BUNDLE FIVE

Oh! We celebrate our coming
When we hear a newborn cry
And we agonize our leaving
With a strained and painful sigh
As the spirit soars the heavens
And renews itself on high
Once more we celebrate our coming
When we hear a newborn cry

I retied the gold ribbon around the remembrances of Maggie and placed them back in the trunk. As I went to pick up the next bundle of papers, my hand was coaxed to the opposite side of the trunk and directly over a cloth bag. I lifted it out of the trunk, and I smiled at what I saw.

It was a hand-sewn satchel, made out of square patches of soft cotton that closed with a drawstring. Each square brought to life a different Mother Goose nursery rhyme, and together created a wonderful collage of children at play. The sack was heavier than the paper bundles and seemed to hold objects rather than letters. I was tired and hungry, and I had the urge to return the bag to the trunk until the next day, but my curiosity was unwilling to let me do that. I sensed the need to discover the secret contents of this bag without delay, so I tucked it under my arm and walked down the steps to the kitchen.

It was a bright day, and the sun was easing its way through the windows. Even though a light snow was on the ground, the sun held the promise of taming the chill in the spring air. In another month, the remains of winter would melt away. I placed the bag on the old wooden kitchen table, filled the teapot with some dried chamomile and boiling water, and then waited a few minutes for the tea to seep. As I glanced at the bag, a childlike feeling filled my heart. The nursery rhyme pictures reminded me of my childhood days. I remembered a big red book of *Aesop's Fables* that sat on the bookshelf in our parlor. My brother, sister, and I would get so excited when my mother would reach for that enchanting book in the evening. We knew that we were getting ready for tales that would lift us into a world of make-believe and carry us as far away as we were willing to go.

Carrying a cup of tea and a honey biscuit, I moved toward the table. I untied the drawstring and stretched apart the puckered opening. Inside, I saw three objects that were bound in different colored ribbons. One by one, I removed them from the bag.

The first one was a small ceramic plate, and it was tied with a light green ribbon. I loosened the bow and held up the plate. It was dark brown, and a picture of a white daisy was hand painted in the center. On the other side, there was an inscription. It said, "To mother, Love Emma." Below Emma's name, age eight was written in pencil.

A red ribbon, which easily unraveled, bound the second object. A small wooden frame, that bordered a watercolor picture of a teddy bear that was wearing a big hat and tilting sideways, presented itself. In the bottom left corner, I could make out the words, "Love, Olivia." On the back of the picture, age ten was written.

The last item was a piece of blue construction paper. It was decorated with different shapes of uncooked pasta and formed a picture of a small hand. This was secured with a blue ribbon. When I untied it, two small pieces of pasta fell from the picture on to the floor. With care, I picked them up and returned them to their original space. The owner of this treasure was Lilly, and she printed her name at the bottom of the page. The "L" and the "y" were backwards. Age five was written under her name.

As I placed each treasure out on the table, I started to recall my meeting with the grown women that were once these little girls...Emily's little girls.

I had met her daughters at the estate closing when I bought the house. I remember that while the lawyers were busy arranging the paperwork, the women invited me to have lunch with them. They all introduced themselves and told me a little about their lives. I remember, we all laughed because

Emma said that because she was the firstborn, she would go first.

She looked like a graceful and kind woman, and carried herself with pride. I could remember that she wore a beautiful light green jewel that hung from a silver chain around her neck. It almost matched the color of the green ribbon that secured the little daisy plate she painted. She told me that she graduated from a small woman's college and pursued a career in medical research. Most of her life's work was studying new treatments for childhood cancers. After she retired, she continued to volunteer at the Children's Hospital. She and her husband, Thor, live in New England. They have two daughters, Sarah and Alexandria. Both are married and have children of their own. Sarah is a nurse and lives in San Diego. Alexandria, a published writer, lives in Philadelphia.

Olivia was the middle daughter. When I met her, she appeared spirited and vibrant, and she displayed liveliness in her step. The casual red and black dress she wore that day reminded me of the red ribbon that slipped from her teddy bear picture, as I lifted it out of the nursery rhyme satchel. Olivia told me that she lives in New York with her husband, James. They have one son, Jacob, who is married and has two sons. He is an architect, living and working on Puget Sound near Seattle. Olivia said that she had been a play writer and director for many years. At a younger age, she did choreography and acting, but she spends most of her time now coaching young actresses for Broadway performances.

The third daughter that I met that day was Lilly. She appeared to be an intelligent woman, yet possessed a humbleness that was unique. She was affectionate and greeted me with a warm hug. I remember her eyes being a beautiful blue color, and when I looked down at the blue ribbon I was still holding, the color matched perfectly. Lilly told me that she is married, and she and her husband, Addison, live in Boston. They have one daughter, Julia, who is not married. Lilly and Julia are physicians, with Julia joining her mother's practice shortly after her residency. Recently, Lilly has retired and is now offering her services as a mentor for young doctors at the university.

These women were in their sixties; yet, they vividly remembered their wonderful childhood and spoke affectionately of those days with Emily and Andrew. I sensed that they were good women, with compassionate hearts. They all chose their life work in careers where they could contribute to the well-being of another individual and make a difference in the lives of their fellow human beings. I heard each one say that even though their formal working years were over, they would continue to reach out to young students and patients, and help them on their way. I sensed in them a love of life, a love of each other, and a love of their fellow man. I heard them speak about their mother and father with love and appreciation, many times, during our visit. They lived with and were taught about a love I was only starting to understand—limitless and unconditional.

It was all so overwhelming. I had met Emily's daughters a few years ago, and now, I was holding the gifts that they made with their little hands, probably over fifty years ago. Sometimes, the human mind cannot grasp what the heart/soul is trying to say, but strange things happen when a spirit seeks to teach a lesson, and the student is ready.

Then, as if a force of energy started to rush through me, a collective consciousness made up of memories, events, facts, and experiences began to connect me with the past. I became fearful and anxious, and tried to divert the path that I thought Emily was preparing for me. Trying to move away from the daydream, I started to clear the dishes from the table and to carry them to the sink. However, the spirit had other plans and became relentless in bringing about the outcome that it had intended.

At first, I heard sounds that seemed to be coming from outside the window. This was impossible, I thought, because no one was around. Then the voices came closer, and I could hear children laughing. When I peered through the window, I saw a woman and three young children outside in the backyard. It was a beautiful summer's day, and the sun was shining. Emily was hanging laundry on a clothesline, and the children were playing hide and seek among the dangling bed sheets. They were laughing and taunting each other, while Emily was pretending to catch them and reprimand them.

Memories unleashed in my mind, and my eyes filled with tears. I remembered the warm sunny days when my sister, brother and I used to play the same game, as my mother hung the wash on the clothesline in our yard. Those cherished days that I let slip away. My brother lived near me in New England for years, but last year, his job transferred him and his family to Florida. Caught in this memory, I felt sad that I rarely spent time with them when they were here. Every summer, he would invite me to the beach with his family, and I never made time to go with them. There was always an excuse for not sharing the time. My sister and her family also lived close. She would take walks in the evening and always ask me to join her, but my busy life was just another excuse that kept us separate and distant.

The need to change my life was all I could think about.

When I looked outside again, I saw another vivid scene. Emily and the children were all sitting under a big shady maple tree with a picnic basket and having lunch in their backyard. They were smiling and talking, when Andrew walked up to them. They looked so loving together. It seemed like he had just stopped for a short visit on the way to see an ill patient, for he was carrying his black medical bag. He spent his life helping and giving to other people.

My thoughts moved elsewhere. More times than I could count, I turned away from people that could have used my help. I chose not to give. I forgot how to care.

In that moment, I heard a deafening sound, and I realized how different my life could be. I didn't want any more regrets. I wanted to make a difference. The body would make the effort, but I knew that it was my spirit that would have to unleash the power. Looking at Emily and her family, I began to pray to a God that would give me what I needed to make the changes.

The voice within me diminished from a screaming to a whisper. Filled with emotion, I closed my eyes, and I began to cry. I cried for so many things...so many things that happened in the past.

When I opened my eyes, the window above the kitchen sink was still open, and a cool night breeze was coming through. Looking out this time, the only vision I saw was a full moon, reflecting the snow on the ground.

All was quiet outside and within my soul.

Emily's remembrances from the children were in front of me. I retied the ribbons and started to place the little gifts back in the bag, when my hand touched some papers that were tucked in a pocket of the lining. They were a collection of diplomas and certificates that marked each daughter's graduation and life accomplishments. They were bound with a piece of yarn, and a poem was the first thing I saw.

GRADUATION DAY

Has it been worth it? Can one truly say?
Perhaps you will find the answers, on graduation day

You look for your purpose, quite a journey, it's true
But how do you find it? What is it you do?

Do you search volumes? Or ask friends over time?
Do you sit and ponder over glasses of wine?

The task is not easy, there is much hidden from view
But I'll tell you a secret, your purpose is within you

I still seek the answers, and I'm halfway through life
The answers get clearer, with each happiness and strife

So a gift I will give you that will start you on your way
In finding your purpose, this I will say

Don't take credit or blame, if it's not what you've done
Because in taking this step, you will always have won

Always tell the truth, as simply as you can
Live on the edge, but don't forget a plan

Be open to the dance, with wildness and charm
And hold tightly to a hand, without binding an arm

Remember to laugh as hardily as you will
And it's okay to cry, or let your heart be still

I know I have learned a big part of a day
Is giving to others, and listening to what they say

You'll meet lots of people, who will come and will go
and some make a difference, a friendship will grow

Make mistakes by the millions, learn from each one
The education you get will be the best under the sun

For the bad that may come, may not be bad after all
Just a friendly reminder, for you to stand tall

And the last piece I offer is the most important I share
To never miss the opportunity to tell someone you care

This day I give advice to you, by all means, not a cure
But it's a gift worth its giving, for it is simple and pure

There is one thing I'm sure of, each time I look at you
There is a glow that is exceptional, in all that you do

You have goodness pouring from your heart, your soul
Even when you're weary, when the day takes its toll

The puzzle unravels, life's answers come in parts
Just glue them together, and let them rest in your heart

For there is that one day, somewhere…down the line
When your purpose is known, living one day at a time

I love you my daughter, my child you will always be
Although a beautiful young woman before me I see

Happy Graduation Day—My Sweet Daughter
Look inside and you will find
The answers to your questions, all in God's time

It was written on a piece of old parchment paper in the most beautiful calligraphy I had ever seen. It was signed: Love forever....Mother. It was dated three different times, which made me think that Emily had presented this poem to each daughter on her graduation day.

Dear Mother,

Thank you for being so inspirational and so you–I love you. When I needed you, you were always there because you cared. You loved me even in my most difficult times and for that, I am grateful. You never stopped encouraging me to work hard and follow my dream. Thank you for the love support and staying by my side when I needed you and even when I thought I didn't need you. You applauded all my achievements and you believed in me when it was hard for me to believe in myself. I love you and thank you for being there through my fears, hopes, tears and laughter. I appreciate all that you are. I love you forever.

Mother,

You have influenced my life in many ways. Remember our early morning walks on the beach we would talk and laugh and watch the sun come up. Being so close to you, seemed to take away all my fears. You are an important part of my life and I will always keep a special place in my heart for you. You taught me how to trust myself and love myself and love others. You always been best to me. Thank you, mother, for sharing all the milestones in my life. You were always there for me. Thank you for loving and guiding me and believing in me. The relationship we have will continue to be treasured. I think about you every day. I love you with all my heart.

Dearest Mother,

I love you to the moon and back. I'm sending you tons of hugs and kisses for all your love and for helping me through some the toughest weeks at school. You helped me reach my dream. I could barely see them. I thank you for your warm heart that always reached out to me. I treasure our times together. I carry your encouragement with me all the time and I feel your warm arms wrapping around me when I am exhausted and lie down at night to sleep. I want to tell you what a wonderful mother you are and how special you are to me.

I will always love you.

Clipped to the poem were three short notes. They were addressed to Emily and signed by each daughter.

The first note was from Emma, dated July 8.

Mother,

You have influenced my life in many ways. Remember our early morning walks on the beach, when we would talk and laugh and watch the sun come up. Being so close to you seemed to take away all my fears. You are an important part of my life, and I will always keep a special place in my heart for you. You taught me how to trust myself, and love myself, and love others. You always saw the best in me. Thank you, Mother, for guiding me and sharing all the milestones in my life. You were always there for me. Thank you for loving me and believing in me. The relationship we have will always be treasured. I think about you every day. I love you with all my heart... Emma

The next note was from Olivia, dated August 19.

Dear Mother,

Thank you for being so inspirational and so you. I love you. When I needed you, you were always there for me because you cared. You loved me even in my most difficult times, and for that, I am grateful. You never stopped encouraging me to work hard and follow my dreams. Thank you for being so strong and staying by my side when I needed you, and even when I thought I didn't need you. You applauded all my achievements, and you believed in me when it was hard for me to believe in myself. I love you and thank you for being there through my fears, hopes, tears, and laughter. I appreciate all that you are. I love you forever... Olivia

The last note was from Lilly, dated September 4.

Dear Mother,

I love you to the moon and back. I'm sending you tons of hugs and kisses for all of your loving support, and for helping me through some of the toughest weeks at school. You helped me reach for the stars when I could barely see them. I thank you for your warm heart that always reached out to me. I treasure our times together. I carry your encouragement with me all the time, and I feel your prayers coming to me when I am exhausted and lie down at night to sleep. I want to tell you what a great mother you are and how special you are to me.

I will always love you... Lilly

The letters from her daughters were such a tribute to her, and although I never humanly knew Emily, I felt a warm love for her. There was a bond between her daughters and her, and I believe that even though there were times when they looked in different directions, they never left go of each other's hand, or heart.

Gently, I placed the diplomas and letters back into the pocket of the Mother Goose satchel and pulled the drawstrings tightly closed.

It was late evening, and I wanted to return the bag to the attic before I went to sleep for the night. As I started to climb the stairs, I stopped. Looking down at the bag, I tenderly ran my hand across the nursery rhyme pictures....Reverently, I bowed my head and placed a kiss on this treasure.

BUNDLE SIX

The spirit chooses a body
And the human form we take
We are born into a family
For the journey we're to make
The family offers comfort
They give freely for love's sake
The spirit chooses a body
For the journey it's to make

Because the attic lighting was poor this time of evening, I decided to light the kerosene lamp and carry it with me to return the satchel to the trunk. It was quiet, and the night provided a peaceful feeling, as the glow from the lamp forced my shadow to walk up the steps ahead of me. I placed the lamp and the bag on the floor, as I raised the cover of the trunk. I promised myself that I would return the satchel and close the trunk for the night. After all, the day had been filled with the unexpected, and I wanted to return to my bedroom and reflect on the happenings.

As I placed the bag gently on top of the other bundles, a book, that looked very familiar, caught my attention. I lifted it out of the trunk and brought it closer to the lamp. The cover was worn and faded, but from what I could see, it closely resembled the book that my grandmother, Angelina, gave to me before she died. My grandmother was of Italian descent, and the book she gave to me was the Bible, written in Italian. She brought it with her from Italy when she came to America with my grandfather, a long time ago. Holding the book from the trunk in one hand, and the lamp in the other, I walked across the attic and opened the cedar chest where I stored all the family remembrances. An eerie feeling ran through my body when I saw my grandmother's Bible lying in the cedar chest, directly on top of her old black shawl. It was identical to the one I held in my hand. Sitting down on a small stool, I placed the books on my lap. I couldn't believe it. I was holding two identical Bibles that were both written in Italian. Inside the front cover of my Bible, my grandmother's name, Angelina, was written. Calabria, the village in Italy where she lived, was written under her name. Inside the front cover of the Bible I found in Emily's trunk, the name, Lucia, was written. It also had Calabria written under her name, and at the bottom of the page was the inscription: "To Emily, I love you, Mama."

Was it possible that my grandmother and Emily's mother were from the same place in Italy? Was it possible that they knew each other? Was this one more connection between the spirit of Emily and me? I felt like my imagination was creating a fantasy that didn't exist. The thoughts were bizarre. My experiences so far with Emily's spirit held meaning for me, and I did not want to disturb this journey by inventing something that was unreal. I was looking at two matching books with a common thread that linked them to Calabria. I had nothing else. Nothing, at least, that would support an association between my grandmother and Emily's mother. At this point, I assumed that I would never know the answers to these questions and started to dismiss the whole notion of any connection between them. I was ready to put the books back into their resting places, when I noticed that both books were marked in the same spot. When I opened each of the Bibles to the marked pages, the psalm, "The Lord is My Shepherd," appeared. Although I could not read Italian, I recognized the words because it was my gandmother's favorite psalm, and she would read it to us when we would visit her on Sundays. Was it just a coincidence that it was also marked in this other Bible? The bookmarkers were beautiful. The one in my grandmother's Bible was a lovely painted image of Saint Lucia. The marker in the other Bible was a picture of an angel, done in needlepoint. What I read next was incredible. On the angel marker, beneath the picture, was written: "God be with you always, Lucia...Love, Angelina."

My God! They did know each other. As I held both of the markers, my hands started to tremble. To think that these two women could have been friends in Italy was beyond what my mind could grasp. I searched for a reason, but logic turned into faith. I believed, with all my heart, that Emily was the greatest teacher I ever had. She knew what my spirit needed to understand before I did, and she was chosen to deliver the message to me through a mysterious chain of events. Finding the Bibles was just one more sign. She knew I still had doubts. Perhaps, by allowing me to uncover a connection that existed between our loved ones a long time ago, she was affirming and strengthening my belief in this journey with her. The love I held for her, and trust I had in her, consumed my entire being.

Doubt was being replaced with faith, and what I believed to be fantasy was, at this moment, accepted as real.

Suddenly, the kerosene lamp started to flicker, and my eyes started to burn. At first, I thought the lamp fuel was getting low, and the fumes were irritating them. I wiped my eyes, attempting to clear my vision, but they were being drawn to a large old trunk that was sitting on the other side of the attic. It was the trunk that my grandmother brought with her on her voyage from Italy to America. As my vision cleared, I began to see two young women sitting on that trunk. They were talking and laughing in Italian, and enjoying each other's company. I never learned to speak or understand the Italian language; yet, I knew everything that they were saying. One woman was getting married and leaving for America, and the other woman was going to follow with her husband in a year or two. They promised to remember and love each other. I heard them say that they would be friends forever. They were young and beautiful, and wore long attractive dresses. Their hair was tucked under wide-rimmed hats. I looked closer. One woman looked like my grandmother, only younger, and she was giving the other woman a book just like the one she held in her hand. I could hear her say that it would protect her on her journey to America. The other woman gave her a picture in return that my grandmother placed into her book. I saw them hug each other, and then I heard them promise that they would see each other again.

I blinked my eyes, and when I opened them, the images were gone. I was saddened, for I wanted to embrace the vision a little longer; yet, I was incredibly content because I felt that I was given yet another sign that finding Emily's trunk was not an accident. There were times on this journey that I doubted it all. Sometimes I felt that the fleeting apparitions were caused by exhaustion from years of intensive concentration on my work, and somehow the restful sabbatical was unleashing these delusions. Now, with the deep peace and quiet affirmation that I felt within me, I knew that was not true. I believed that this journey was prepared for me lifetimes ago; however, until the student is ready, the teacher lies silently awaiting the hour of awareness. Therefore, when the time is right, the lessons are given; thus, when the spirit is ready, the lessons are learned.

As with any journey, the first steps are the most extraordinary, and tonight, my uncertainties have been resolved, and my fears put to rest.

I closed the Bibles and gently placed mine back in the cedar chest, on top of my grandmother's shawl. I carried Emily's over to the trunk and opened her Bible one last time. A folded map was tucked in the back flap of the book and showed a hand-drawn sketch of the village of Calabria. Also tucked in the flap was a letter. Carefully, I unfolded it and started to read.

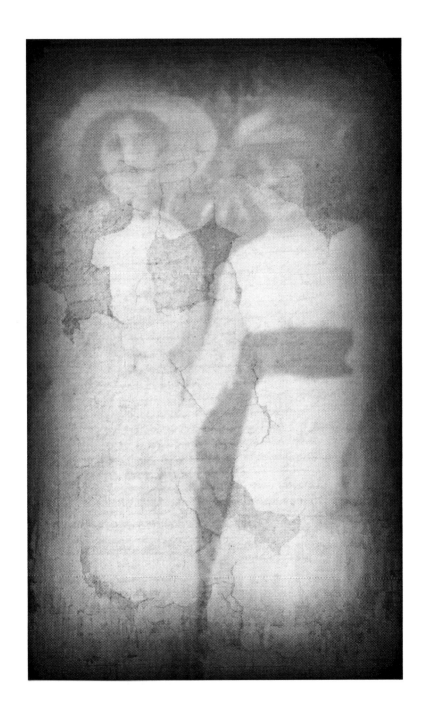

Dear Emily,

March 14

Today, on your special day, I want to tell you how proud I am to be your mama. I remember the day you came into my life; the day you were born. I remember feeling scared and wondering how I would care for you. I didn't know the first thing about being a mother. My bambino, you were so tiny and helpless, but so easy to love. I just let love lead the way.

Sometimes that love was in laughter. Sometimes that love was in tears, but through it all, we learned together and we grew together. It seems like just yesterday you were a little girl, and today, I am looking at a beautiful young woman. You have given me so many wonderful memories, and I am proud of you in so many magnificent ways. The world stands before you awaiting your embrace. Emily, you are confident and loving, and you will do well in any path that you wish to explore. Today, you will walk on your own; however, if you should need me, I am never far away, and I will stand by you always. Remember that no matter where you are, I will always be thinking of you and loving you more than life itself.

They say as one grows older, the eyesight dims, but the vision clears, and as I look back on all my life's accomplishments, please believe that my most treasured achievement was becoming your mother.

I pray that you are given the wisdom, understanding, and strength; the confidence, courage, and compassion; the dignity and faith to make decisions that are good for you; and decisions that will take you to your highest good and learning.

May God be with you everywhere you go, and may you make every day that you awake a special day for yourself and another that needs your help. I think of you often and love you always. Be well.

Mama

I heard the old grandfather clock in the living room strike midnight. The kerosene light dimmed from lack of oil, and I knew it was time to sleep. I returned the letter to the back cover of the Bible and lovingly placed it in the trunk. As I walked down the steps to my bedroom, I thought how Emily came from a long ancestry of loving spirits. I smiled. No wonder she was chosen to deliver the lesson of giving and loving to a heart and soul that knew little about it.

Descending from the attic, I reached the last step. As I opened the door that led to my room, the kerosene lamp started to dim even more, and I could feel Emily's spirit fading with the dying flame.

BUNDLE SEVEN

The roar of the mighty river
The trickle of the stream
The flight of the soaring eagle
The gliding hawk on wing
Aware that the mighty spirit
Inspires the human dream
As the roar of the mighty river
Enchants the gliding hawk on wing

Oh! Little caterpillar
Oh! Gracious butterfly
One clings to the earth
And the other to the sky
We need to learn to walk first
Before we learn to fly
Oh! Little caterpillar
Oh! Gracious butterfly

I awoke well before dawn with the plan to spend most of the day pruning and weeding in the herb garden. With autumn approaching, it was a chore that needed to be done, and it was usually neglected when I was teaching at school. With a cup of coffee in hand, I headed for the herb garden.

When I had the time, I always loved to sit on the old, wooden bench in the morning with a cup of strong, hot coffee, and watch the sun come up over the mountain. I never tired of seeing its brilliance slowly inching its way upward over the peak until it took its place of honor in the universal sky. It announced a new day and a new beginning.

Today, I wanted to escape to the quiet of the herb garden and take some time away from the attic and the trunk. I wanted to mull over the months since I started my sabbatical, and try to understand the strange happenings that continued to preoccupy my mind, not to mention, transform my heart and my soul. Although I was convinced that the events I witnessed were not a coincidence, I needed time to put the pieces of this puzzle together and understand its timing and purpose. However, what I believed to be my decision to avoid the attic, I later realized had nothing to do with me and everything to do with the spirit's pull in the direction of the herb garden.

The small stone summer kitchen sat to the left of the house. It was a suitable shelter for my garden tools when not in use, and for my straw hat that protected me from the heat of the sun. Rolling back the old wooden door, I walked over to my straw hat that hung on an old nail on the far wall. I was about to put it on when I remembered something. When I returned the Bible to the trunk, I saw a straw hat lying on the floor of the trunk. It was the last thing in there, and I decided to wait for another time to take a look at it.

Although I had promised myself to avoid the trunk, my curiosity got the best of me, and once again, I headed to the attic. The wide brim hat rested on the floor of the trunk. Unlike mine, this hat was tattered and worn, and the white chiffon ties, which were threaded through the sides, were yellowed with age. I put the hat on my head and secured the ties. As I did this, an envelope that fell from the cap landed on the attic floor. I picked it up and removed a hand-sketched picture of the herb garden with a short description of all the flowers and herbs that were planted there. Had Emily drawn this and placed it in her straw hat? For what reason, I was not sure; however, the sketch that I found looked like the same herb garden that I cared for since I bought the house. With her hat on my head, and her drawing in my hand, I hurried outside.

The herb garden never looked more beautiful than it did today. The sun was shining brilliantly, as it flashed its rays on the golden sundial that sat on a thick piece of weathered wood directly in the middle of the garden. Stone paths that pointed north, south, east, and west divided the garden into four separate parts. An old stone wall surrounded the entire garden, and a stone bank barn was located across from it.

Each section of the garden contained an assortment of flowers and herbs, and today, the aroma from them seemed stronger than usual. Mother Nature was a dependable gatekeeper. She kindly watched over the perennials from year to year, as they faithfully returned each spring after the winter snow disappeared. The herb garden was identical to the sketch that Emily drew. As I followed the outline through the garden, each herb and flower was almost in the same place.

Chamomile was plentiful, and the small delicate, daisy-like flower was right up front. Under the drawing and the name of the herb, there was a notation. Emily jotted down a meaning for each one. Next to the word Chamomile, she wrote *understanding*. Lavender and the Rosemary were planted behind the Chamomile. According to the note, one represented *dedication* and the other *commemoration*. She drew small circles on the paper that resembled the stone path. She planted Parsley for *laughter*, Marjoram for *pleasure*, and Sage for *strength* and *well-being*. She had written *valor* next to Borage, and *honesty* next to the Bee Balm. The Thyme and the Tarragon were tucked into the corner of the garden next to the stone wall. Thyme meant *courageous*, and Tarragon stood for *attachment*. The Mint and Aloe grew in abundance, and occupied a part of the garden all by themselves. Emily described them as *medicinal* and *healing*. Except for the Columbine, all the other flowers had their particular place. She must have loved the Columbine the best because it bloomed in all colors and grew almost anywhere it wanted to. Next to it, she wrote….*My special flower*. On the far end of the garden, the Red Roses bloomed, and when I looked down at her drawing, the words *Andrew* and *Love* were written next to it. Next to the Rose, the Blue Iris grew. She described the Iris as *innocent*. She noted the Violet for *humility*, and the Yarrow, which grew on the opposite side of the Rose, was for *vigor*. The Black Eyed Susan and the Pink Coneflower grew next to the east wall along with the Marigold and Zinnia that I replanted each year. They gave me a sense of remembrance. Perhaps because they stayed in the garden the longest and were usually the last flower to leave when the first frost appeared. Before the winter snow set in, one could see a small tiny yellow bird balancing himself on the dried tip of the Coneflower and nourishing himself with the seeds. On the bottom of the page, there were recipes for herb butters, herb oils, vinegars, and mint jelly. She also had instructions on making scented candles and dried herbal wreaths.

Sitting on the wooden bench, I looked around the garden with an admiration that given more time could have easily turned to worship; however, I was distracted by the unusual alignment of the sundial for this time of day. Moving in its direction, I looked down at my watch. The time read 10:15 a.m. When I was out in the garden, I always liked to compare the time on the sundial to the clock time, and without fail, it always matched exactly. Today was different. This time when I read the dial, I was set back by what I saw. The glistening structure in front of me, oddly, pointed to 6 p.m. In disbelief, I rechecked my watch. Once again, it read 10:15 a.m. The sundial did not budge. It steadfastly pointed to 6 p.m....

Then I saw her. It was a face that I have come to know so well. The spirit was sitting on an old wooden bench on the far side of the herb garden, and with a gentle wave of her hand, she beckoned me to come to her. She appeared old and frail. She wore a blue print dress that was partially covered with a light blue apron and had brown monk-like sandals on her feet. Her hair was gray and pinned into a bun. On her head, she wore a straw hat that resembled the one I found in the trunk; the same hat that I was now wearing.

In the past, I became fearful when Emily would appear, but this time it was different. I felt myself drawing closer to her. She stared at me with those same beautiful eyes that endeared me to her in the beginning. Common sense raced against emotion. Reality ran contrary to fantasy, and then suddenly, I was calm, and my doubt, once again, was gently transformed into belief. She reached for my hand as I approached her, and although I did not feel a human touch, a warm feeling filled my being, and I knew I wanted to stay in her presence.

We sat for a while in silence, and in those moments, which seemed like time without end, the years started to rewind. Visions from my life passed before me. Decisions, regrets, achievements, and failures seemed to collide. I struggled to separate the good from the bad until I realized that I didn't have to do that anymore. There was a reason it all happened the way it did, and I felt at peace.

She whispered an invitation to walk with her and motioned toward the path behind the barn that led into the woods. I knew the way so well. It was a path that I loved to walk throughout the seasons. Each special time of the year, it displayed its own natural beauty and majesty. At the end of the path, there was an old bench that had been there when I bought the house. I always believed it was a magical old bench. Many times, I would sit there with my questions or worries, and when I would leave, those questions seemed to all have answers, and much of the uneasiness disappeared. It was on that bench that I finally decided to take the long anticipated sabbatical.

At first, I was frightened by Emily's invitation because it reminded me of the Biblical story of Enoch that was told at my grandmother's funeral. As the story goes, each day God would knock on Enoch's door and invite him to walk with Him. Enoch loved to walk and talk with the Lord. One day, God decided that Enoch's work on this earth was over and wanted to take him to his eternal home. So, as he did every day, God visited Enoch and invited him to walk with Him; only this time, as they walked and talked together, God led Enoch to his heavenly home. Was this what was happening to me? Was I being led to my heavenly home?

"Walk with me, Sophia." I heard her say in a very soft voice. "Complete the journey with me and discover yourself....we have come so far."

She got up from the bench and started to walk toward the path. I slowly followed. As I passed the herb garden, I noticed a small caterpillar moving across the stone toward the Mint and the Aloe. There was probably a time, I thought, when this little caterpillar believed his life was over, but instead, he turned into a gracious butterfly. As I turned the corner by the barn, I felt like that little caterpillar whose form was about to change.

Then, I saw Emily standing in the clearing. She was patiently waiting for me.

BUNDLE EIGHT

Isn't it strange that we take for granted
The air that we breathe
The light that we see
The sky that hangs above us
And the earth under our feet
Isn't it strange that we assume we will have
Another day to play
Another night to rest
Another bright sunny sky
Another clear star-filled night
Isn't it strange to think that we will
Scoop one more shovel of winter snow
Plant one more spring perennial
Cut one more yard of summer grass
Rake one more pile of fall leaves
Isn't it strange to believe
That time will go on……..

As we started to walk down the path, the spirit within me enmeshed with the spirit that was sent to teach me, and the journey started ....When the student is ready, the teacher will appear.

Like Enoch and the Lord, Emily and I started to walk, and she began to speak.

"Sophia," she said, "we are all born into this world with a spirit that is honorable and forward moving. Because of this, we all have the ability to reach the higher wisdom within us. In order for us to do this, we are given special lessons to learn and a lifetime to do it. It is handed to us in a cluster of pieces that we are expected to fit together like a puzzle. The finished puzzle is comprised of the lessons that have been chosen for our spirit to embrace. Then we take on a human body and come to Earth to understand them and learn them."

Emily and I continued to walk the path. She said, "Some people discover their lessons and accomplish them without difficulty. Others go through their entire lives and never look for them, and, therefore, never discover them. These spirits are given another chance, at another time, in another life to try and understand their lessons again. Then there are spirits like you, Sophia, who want to discover what the lessons are and really want to learn them; however, when they try, they are blocked by their free will, which is given to all of us when we take on our human form. They make decisions based on earthly influences and rewards that take them off their true path and place them on a different course. Human beings, like you, have extraordinary spirits. They have such an intensely pure desire to learn their lessons and fulfill their destiny, but unfortunately, they lose their way. These are the souls that need extraordinary means to get them back on their predetermined path and recapture the reason for their being." She lovingly smiled at me, "You are one of those special people that were chosen to be helped along the way by a spiritual teacher. I have been chosen to be that teacher because I have lived and learned through many lifetimes and have come close to perfection in the lessons of unconditional loving, caring, and giving. As you probably know from our insightful journey so far, these are the lessons your spirit was predestined to learn. I have been sent to help you see with new eyes and put the puzzle back together.

"As you have discovered, my name was Emily in life. I was a teacher when I lived here, and through a chain of events, I have led you to this house at a time when you are aware and ready to be guided back on your course. I was sent to meet you on your journey and offer you an unexpected turn toward a new path that will add meaning to your life. This is not an end, Sophia, rather a beginning.

"You see, we are really all spiritual beings and have worn many human guises in different lifetimes in order for the spirit to experience many trails and grow more perfect. Because of this, we are part of everyone that surrounds us, and everything that goes on in this world. We are connected to one spirit, and to each other; therefore, the events that happen to one individual affect another in some way. One time or another, you were the young mother with her new child. You were the brilliant student in the classroom. You were the Trappist monk tending his vegetable garden, as well as the scientist in his laboratory, who has just succeeded with his experiment. However, Sophia, you were also the disabled child in school. You were the drunkard lying on the street corner. You were the warrior at the front line of battle, and you were also the old woman dying alone in a sanatorium. There is a common, fragile strand that joins our spirits together. We are part of all humanity, and as long as we remember this, we remain on our true path. It is when we separate ourselves, isolate ourselves, and start to lock in on just the things that we want, we forget what we are supposed to be doing, who we are supposed to be, and the lessons our spirit came to Earth to learn. We become hermits and loners, who are off in a world of our own. That is what happened to you. The pieces to the puzzle got scrambled when you became self-absorbed in your life, and you worked only for your own glory and external, material rewards. You were running through life so fast that it became a race, rather than the journey it was meant to be. Every once in awhile, you would give some thought to a different way of living, but you soon fell back into the same trap. You became frustrated, discouraged, anxious, and detached. Your deeds were selfish and not genuine. It was your free will run riot. You kept following the same roadmap and driving down the same road; a road, that no matter how many times you traveled it, would show you the same sights and take you to the same destination."

She put her arm through mine. "I was sent to you to invite you to take another road. The solution to change is simple: If what you are doing is causing you great unhappiness and discontent, then stop doing it, and do something else. Take another road, and if you find that you have become unhappier and are filled with more discontent, then you know that you went in the wrong direction. You don't have to ride the train into the wall. Turn it around and go the other way."

I started to cry. "Why did I not do this sooner? How could I have been so blind?" I said. She took my hand. "Sophia, when you alienate yourself and stop trying, life becomes meaningless. It becomes painful. However, pain can be your greatest gift. From pain comes wisdom, and many people use that pain to open new doors for themselves. Human beings don't make mistakes, Sophia, because of what they do. They make mistakes because of what they don't do…..They don't do enough."

The bench at the path's end was visible, and we continued to walk toward it. "Should we not have something to show for our stay here on Earth?" Emily said, "Should we return to the Universe without finishing our lessons? Many do. You still have your free will, and you can choose to ignore this gift I bring to you. I have left you messages in the old trunk to start you on your way to a new life of loving and giving. I can tell you that your life will become more satisfying if you heed the call. You will become a whole person, and you will never want to, or be able to, go back to where you were. A butterfly cannot return to a caterpillar, nor does it want to. Once a spirit learns the lessons he needs to learn, he can never move backwards, only ahead. When you move forward, your old life will be so far behind you that you will hardly remember what that life was like."

She stopped and picked a fragrant flower, a Columbine, and handed it to me. "It will take hard work, and the work will be continuous. It will take a day-by-day type of living, and in this way, you will fully live all the days of your life. Life will become simple, and the more you understand what is going on, the more you will start to follow the way that you were meant to live, and not the way you have lived before. Take the risk. That is the only way you will become brave and courageous, and you will need bravery and courage to overcome the human will."

As we reached the bench at the end of the path, she motioned for me to sit down. Evening was upon us, and the sky was darkening. The wind started to blow, and the tall trees waved back and forth, releasing a soothing breeze on us. Once more, she took my hand. "You have a beautiful passion for life, Sophia. Look for the things that are closest to your heart and soul; the gifts you were born with. Take your knowledge, abilities, and skills that this earthly life has taught you, and give it all to every person you meet. You will be surprised what the Universe will give back to you. I caution you to leave behind the one thing that has not served you well in the past, and that is your ego. You are a strong woman, Sophia. I have watched you for a long time. Today, I offer you a simple lesson in humble, unreserved love for yourself and others. Remember where you have come from, and believe in where you are going. I wish you well."

As she said those last words, I felt her hand slipping out of mine and reaching for a hand that was outstretched to her. It was Andrew, and he was walking in her direction. He appeared from nowhere and sat down next to her. She kissed him, and he lovingly put his arms around her. She nuzzled closer to him. It was almost like they were not aware of my presence, until Emily turned to me and motioned me up the path, as if she were sending me away.

Unsure of what I should do, I started walking back to the house. Making my way up the path, I could still hear them talking and playfully laughing with each other. Suddenly, the sounds stopped. Uncertain of what I would find, I slowly turned around. I could not believe my eyes. The bench was empty. Emily and Andrew were no longer there.

Saddened, I continued walking toward the house. Then, I started to run. I pulled the straw hat off my head, ran into the house, and hurried up the attic steps. Putting the hat back in the trunk, I checked to see if all the bundles were there and in the same order that I had found them. With that done, I closed the trunk.

Tears ran down my face as I secured the leather straps. I never wanted to separate myself from this treasure, although now I knew that the real treasure was no longer in the trunk. It was within me. What remained in the trunk were cherished family memories. These belonged to her daughters.

The following day, I searched for the phone number that Emily's daughter had given to me at the sale of the house. The phone rang three times, and a voice that sounded like Emma answered. She was pleasant and said she was happy to hear from me. I explained to her that when I was cleaning the attic, I found an old trunk that was hidden behind a partition, and I thought it belonged to her mother. I told her that I took the liberty of opening it, and I found it was filled with family memories that she and her sisters may like to have. She was thrilled with the news, and we soon scheduled a time and place that we would meet.

The following week, I delivered the trunk to her. When she saw it, she smiled and told me that this trunk was always very special to her mother. She remembered that Mother always kept it filled with gifts and cards from the family. The last time she saw it was the year before her mother died. On one of their visits, she asked Lilly and Olivia to carry it down from the attic for her and put it in her bedroom. They did just as she asked. Emma was silent, and there were tears in her eyes. She put her hand on top of the trunk and held it there for a while, like she had just recovered a treasure that had been lost for a long time. I did not intrude on her silence.

In time, we started to speak. She thanked me, hugged me, and as I was getting ready to leave, I thought of something that I wanted to ask her. I wanted to know if she would be willing to share with me something about her mother. I explained to her that because of the warmth and beauty I found in the home and in the gardens, I believed her mother to be a woman out of the ordinary. I told her I was curious about the details of her mother's death and burial. She smiled and took my arm, and we walked to the little diner on the corner. Ordering tea and honey biscuits, we sat together in deep conversation.

She said that each day, she, Olivia, or Lilly would telephone their mother to see if she was all right. Every year in the fall, they always planned a weekend together, and that day, they were headed to her house for that special time. When they arrived, their mother was not there. At first, they were concerned. Then they thought she might have taken a walk while she was waiting for them, so they decided to check the path that she walked every day. She told me that there used to be an old wooden bench at the end of the path, and that her mother and father would go there together to be alone. "We all started walking in the direction of the bench," Emma said, "and we started recalling the times when we were growing up. Sometimes, we could not find our parents in the house, so we would run down the path laughing and screaming, and there they would be, sitting on the bench with their arms open to us.

"That day was different." She continued, "As we approached the bench, we knew something was wrong, and we all hurried to our mother. She was sitting there, but had fallen to her side. When we reached her, we found that she had died." Tears came to Emma's eyes. "We all loved her so much. She always took such good care of our family, and she taught us the important things in life. She was our inspiration." Taking her hand, I sat with her in silence, and I could feel her sadness. She continued. "I remember it was an early fall day. The type of day that you can only experience in New England." She said with an endearing look. "My mother always loved the evening hours. That was when her day's work was done, and she would sit on the bench in the herb garden and have her tea. When my father was alive, he would join her, and they would watch the sun go down while they talked about their day." As she wiped away another tear, she continued. "My mother had a final request. On her death, she asked if we would have her body cremated, and her ashes spread across the herb garden. She wanted us to do it in the evening hours preferably at 6 p.m., because that was the time that my father would usually meet her there." She continued. "So we did as she wished. After a short service in our small-town church, my sisters invited our mother's friends and neighbors to a gathering at my mother's home. It was a beautiful day. There were many heartfelt words and acts of kindness from all who knew her. This woman, who spent her whole life in this little New England town, was loved and respected by all who knew her. The gathering lasted most of the day. As evening approached and all the people left, we found ourselves alone in the house. Together, my sisters and I took the walnut box filled with our mother's ashes, and we walked to the herb garden.

"The sky was overcast, and a light rain started to fall." She said with a smile. "It was almost like our mother had planned it that way. In life, she always loved a cloudy, rainy day, and today, she was returning to the Universe under her favorite sky." Emma said that she could remember it like it was yesterday. "My sisters and I sprinkled our mother's beloved ashes throughout her herb garden at 6 p.m., and we stood solemnly as we watched a gentle rain tuck them gently into the ground." With a peaceful look in her eyes, she told me that they had spent that night in the house, and the next day when they left, they took the memory of their mother and father, and the memory of the wonderful old house from their childhood, with them. They looked for the trunk at that time, but it was nowhere to be found. We finished our tea, and the visit was over. I thanked her; we hugged each other, and we left.

It was noon when I returned home. Filled with sadness for someone I felt I knew all my life, I walked over to the herb garden that Emily loved and gathered a bouquet of the herbs and flowers. In the summer kitchen, I pulled the chiffon tie from the straw hat, bound the flowers together, and, once again, walked to the herb garden.

The sun was shining brightly, and the air was still. I reached the sundial, knelt down, and with a grateful heart, placed the bouquet at the bottom of the wooden post. "I have grown because you have touched me," I whispered.

Suddenly, it was as if unseen hands took the bouquet from mine. I knew them well. They were familiar hands…..the same unseen hands that welcomed me to open the trunk on that fateful day in the attic.

As I got to my feet, a shadow passed in front of me, and a gentle breeze brushed across my face.

The bouquet was gone, and I stood motionless.

The sundial read……. 6 p.m.

EPILOGUE

Several years have passed since that day in the herb garden and since I have last seen Emily. The herbs and flowers continue to grow, and, once again, you can set a watch by the sundial every day. The dance was over….. Emily was gone.

After Emily, my life changed. I was strengthened in purpose, and I had a new understanding in living each day. I found a new way to give and a better way to love. I was eager to move forward in my life and to touch the lives of others around me. To be given this gift was more than a blessing….it was a wonder.

How this all happened, I'm still not sure. As I look back, what appeared to be my accidental discovery of an old trunk was really the hands of fate preparing to offer me a chance to change my life. To this day, I am grateful that I did not turn away, and for reasons that will never be known to me, I am especially grateful for the persistence of a spirit called Emily. Her timing was perfect…..the lesson was seamless, and although we came to the end of the path, the journey for me had just begun. She was my teacher. She was my friend.

As time passed, I missed her more and more. Then I remembered what she taught me, and I started to look for her in the subtle, quiet places of nature where her presence is so strongly connected. In those silent moments, I find her and join her there. It is in that silence that I find my greatest peace. As I walk alone during the day, I could feel her in the sunshine. I feel her warmth as it penetrates my soul…. for she is the sun. I started to join my sister on her evening walks, and I feel Emily's presence in our newfound sharing. Emily is the stars and the moon, and many a night, I gaze at her from the porch rocker, and she sends her light back to me. I no longer run to shelter if I am out in the gentle rain, for it is another place I have learned to meet Emily. I hold my face up to the drops of moisture, for she is the refreshing rain. Every summer, I now look forward to visiting my brother and his family. We go to the beach and have a wonderful time. My brother and I started getting up early in the morning and taking walks on the sand, so that we could see the sun rise over the ocean's edge. At that moment, I could feel the strong presence of Emily, as I watch the waves moving in and out. I know that she is the mighty ocean, and my spirit is renewed in the vastness and beauty that those waters hold. I become especially quiet when the wind starts to whisper in the spring or howl in the winter, for that is yet another voice of Emily calling to me. She is the wind, and although I cannot see her, I know she is there.

On a quiet autumn day, as I watch the timely beauty of a leaf slowly falling from a tree, I hear the message of Emily. I understand the lesson it teaches as it descends to the ground not one second sooner then it is called to do so.......When the student is ready, the teacher will appear.

The following month, my sabbatical ended, and I returned to the classroom at the Women's College to start a new semester. I stood in this classroom many times before and welcomed new students. This time, it was different. My life changed, and all those things that mattered before—reward, pride, ego—were no longer the reasons I was standing there. This time, I was there to make a difference in the lives of these young women that soon would sit before me. I was there to give freely and without condition, simply because the gift was mine to give. If the applause would come, I'm sure I would not hear it. There was a power within me that I could not deny, and I was filled with a peace that surpasses all comprehension and understanding.

Emily gave to me all that she had to give. She offered me a gift to life's deeper meaning. She let me see the world through new eyes and feel the compassion of an open heart. Soon, I would stand in front of these young women with that same offering. I wanted to give them all I had to give, and for the first time, I wanted nothing in return. Emily was patient and gently persistent. Today, I felt blessed with her patience and loving perseverance. Today is an extraordinary day for me.

At the start of a new semester, it was a tradition at our college to meet the students and have the students meet each other. This semester was no exception. When the last student was seated in my classroom, I closed the door. I walked to the center of the room until I came to stand directly in front of the class. I introduced myself. Then I asked each student to do the same, and also present the course of study they were preparing to follow. As each woman said her name, I could feel myself connect with her, and I silently wished each well.

As we moved toward the last seat in the class, my heart, for some unknown reason, started to beat faster. A young woman, with eyes so gentle and loving, rose to her feet. As I looked at her, I felt I knew her from another place. Then suddenly, the sensation of familiarity changed to a feeling of embracing peace. She looked at me and began to speak in a soft voice. A whisper, I recognized from the past........

"I have lived in New England all my life," she said, "and I want to be a teacher." Then with a smile that seemed to touch all in the room, she said......

"My name is Emily."

www.jeannelefevre.com